UGLY GUIDE

TO THE UGLYVERSE

TO MINA

Visit us on the Web! www.randomhouse.com/kids
www.uglydollbooks.com

Educators and librarians, for a variety of teaching tools,
visit us at www.randomhouse.com/teachers

Library of Congress Cataloging-in-Publication Data
Horvath, David.
The ugly guide to the uglyverse /
by David Horvath and Sun-Min Kim—1st ed.   p.   cm.
ISBN 978-0-375-84275-7 (trade)—ISBN 978-0-375-93683-8 (lib. bdg.)
I. Kim, Sun-Min.   II. Title.   PZ7.H79222Ug   2007
2007013352

PRINTED IN SINGAPORE
10 9 8 7 6 5 4 3 2 1   First Edition

UGLY GUIDE

TO THE UGLYVERSE

by David Horvath & Sun-Min Kim

RANDOM HOUSE
NEW YORK

WAGE

MINIMUM
WAGE

BABO

JEERO

ICE-BAT

UGLYDOG

BOP

'N'

BEEP

MOXY

UGLYWORM

GATO
DELUXE

DEER
UGLY

TRAY

CINKO

TARGET

WEDGEHEAD

OX

UGLYDOG

CHUCKANUCKA

PEACO

BIG
TOE

ABIMA

UGLY GHOST

POE

WELCOME TO UGLYTOWN

Never heard of it? You know those parts of the world you may have overheard people telling each other about? Uglytown is nothing like those places. Uglytown is a small part of the larger Uglyverse . . . and a very busy one!

Uglytown is a lot like any other city near you. Only they have robots, restaurants enclosed in staircases, and paranormal-themed shopping centers.

Oh, and for those reading this book in the year 3000: Okay, so you have robots. But not like these! Yours work!

Busy! Uglytown is always on the move.
The citizens of Uglytown have places to
go, people to see, and things to do.

PIRATE FOOD!!

C
O
V
E

MENU
R = 2¢
R! = 5¢
R? = 6¢

THIS SIDE BROKEN

SHIP-IT

ALL IN THE SAME
BOAT COVE·IN

EAT AT R'S!

MY SHIP HAS COME IN!

ENTER
ON other SIDE

SHIP IT!
ON OUR SLOW BOAT!

IF YOU NEED IT SOONER AVOID OUR SCHOONER!

MENU
R!

D

W

ND!!

What kinds of things? Just things. You know. Does Uglytown feel familiar to you? Maybe it's because of the Laundromat for Fish and Toys? Must be!

DRIVER'S LICENSE

HELLO MY NAME IS

WAGE

AGE: OLD ENOUGH
LIKES: YOUR HAIR
DISLIKES: NO JOB
APRON: YES
EXPIRES: SOMEDAY

Wage is a hard worker, just like you.
His dream is to find a job and to do that job
really well. Maybe someday.

I'M WORKIN' HERE!

Wage can be found
working at Price Hike
here in Uglytown.

They don't know he works there, though.
Mostly because he doesn't. Don't tell Wage!
(Or Minimum Wage.)

WAGE LOVES...

HIS FRIENDS · ROBOTS · ICE CREAM · YOU SCREAM

WORKING ZZZZ · HELPING ZZZZ · TOW TRUCKS · TOE TRUCKS

WAGE'S BIG TOW

WAGE'S BIG TOW

MAP

BIG TOW

Wage loves spending his weekends in his
very own tow truck with his best friend, Babo.

COOKiE PERMiT

NAME: BABO
AGE: SMALL
SPECIAL COOKIE SKILL: EATING

Wage's best buddy, Babo, may not be so bright,
but what he lacks in brain power, he makes up
for with love. The love of cookies, that is.

MAKE

BAKE

TAKE

Babo's always got your back, and when
something scary happens, he'll send you a nice
letter from wherever it is he's run away to.

UH-OH

Babo often wonders what would
happen if they stopped making cookies.
It could happen! Right? If you do the
math, it's time to make our own!

2+2

2+2 = 🍪

2+2 =

BABO'S CALCULATIONS

If you want to do something right, it may be
possible that you'll have to do it yourself.
It's also possible that you should ask for help.
Actually, ask for help anyway.
Especially if you're Babo.

SUPER DELUXE TRAIN STATION
& DONUT HOUSE

Everything starts at the Uglytown
Super Deluxe Train Station . . .
except for the train! The very late
citizens of Uglytown make a break
for the office—it's a race against
the clock! (Well, first to the
Donut House, then the office.)

Don't forget the Donut House! The world-famous Uglytown Train Station Donut House is on the way down the escalator, so make up your mind and practice giving your order. There's nothing like having only twenty seconds to order and pay for your donut.

A relaxing way to start your day in Uglytown!

JOBS!

So you're thinking about moving to Uglytown?
Well then, you're going to need to find a job!
There are many to pick from: lowly office
do-nothing, low-level box mover, sailor,
ice-cream cook . . . you name it!

Being the big boss is what everyone wants, but it's not such an easy job! You have to show up a few times a week! Then they make you push all kinds of buttons.

OX AND WEDGEHEAD

Wedgehead and Ox seem to get into trouble
far too often.

They're really good at some things, like magic.
Their best trick is turning your stuff into their stuff.
What they're not so good at is cooking (or cleaning).
They keep the fire department very busy.

UGLY FIREHOUSE

The Ugly Firehouse is home to the bravest of the brave. Every day, these incredible firefighters put on their huge, heavy hats and big, hot coats and put out fires caused by Wedgehead and Ox's attempts at making s'mores.

There are always some Ugly firefighters
sleeping in the firehouse in case there's a fire
somewhere. After two bowls of chili, the fire
seems to be in Wedgehead's tummy tonight!

I WANT
MY
OWN
ROOM!

UGLY HOSPITAL

SICK? PERFECT!

GET WELL

SOONISH

BUT MY TUMMY HURTS!

Sour tummy? We've got you covered! Aches and pains? No problem! A hundred feet tall? Yeah . . . uh, please hold.

The Ugly hospital has the BEST custard in town! They have fruit custard, green bean custard, and custard with little cube things in it. The best part is, while you eat, you get to watch TV (one channel).

DR. FOOL R YOU.

HE'S OK

HE'S NOT

Tray has three brains . . . one per lump.
While Tray may be a smarty, she's been known
to become confused at times. The doctors tell
her it's all in her mind. Just as Tray suspected!

While the hospital custard may taste great, the
$100-per-five-minutes hospital bill may not . . .
so be sure to try Ox and Wedgehead's
ice-cream emergency ambulance!

The folks here in Uglytown are pretty regular.

HOW DO I WORK THIS THING.!?

They go to school.

HEY!!!

U R FIRED X

They go to work.

EX-EXPERT

Which way to the Bank?

They have pets.

Bow wow

They have robots.

And they go
to the mall.

The UGLYTOWN SCHOOL of LEARNING

DUNCE

Let that BE A LESSON TO YOU!

You know how people say "If I wanted to read, I would go to school"?

I Don't GO!

END OF THE ROAD

Well then, let us welcome you to the Uglytown School of Learning! Anyone can attend. All you have to do is be okay with making a fool of yourself and with not having air-conditioning. If you can do that for us, we'll teach you stuff.

ANYONE? ANYONE?

super fancy

DIPLOMA

FOR DOING A-OK

NAME: BIG TOE
AGE: GETTING OLDER
SIZE: BIG
TOES: NONE

Big Toe is very busy, but he's going to take care of everything. Just watch. At first he may seem a little slow . . . until you realize he's always one step ahead. Those donuts you were saving for tomorrow? Gone. Those leftovers from the picnic? Gone.

Big Toe's on top of things!

YEAH, GREAT

This diploma certifies Big Toe as a real smarty.

IT'S FUNNY, I DIDN'T EVEN STUDY!

RESTAURANTS

& CAFES

If you're going to be walking around Uglytown all day, you'll need to eat. We suggest . . . food! There are thousands of restaurants in Uglytown, so we'll break it all down into three groups: super expensive, kinda okay price, and so cheap the pigeons don't want any part of it.

Chez Fancy Pants is a real hot spot. They call it a hot spot because the prices burn a hole in your wallet! The food is really good, but we recommend going for the bread, the water, and the exit if you want to have anything left for, say, buying things.

TAKO HUT

ORDER HERE

TAKO TACO

TAKO SOUP

TAKO CONE

TAKO SHAKE

Tako Hut is one of the most popular octopus-themed restaurants in Uglytown. They don't use real octopus in the food, but the ingredients they do use will make you think of sea life for sure! Everything tastes really fishy!

HMM?

Everyone's least favorite place to eat is 2-Big Burger. They have these really big, juicy burgers that come with free fries and this bubble-based stuff called soda. Nasty, right? Who would eat such a thing?

2-BIG BURGER

Ew!

99¢

OFFICIAL
NO-SWIMMING
PERMISSION SLIP

I FEAR

NAME: CINKO
FEAR: WATER
DISLIKES: ICE
SWIM?: NO WAY

Cinko is afraid of water. Okay, well, Cinko is afraid of a lot of things. But water takes the scary cake. Maybe Cinko doesn't like big waves? See, but then why is Cinko afraid of a little glass of water? So has Cinko ever taken a bath? If this were a scratch-and-sniff book, you wouldn't have to ask. Cinko is sort of okay with ice, and that's a big step. Or he's okay with pictures of ice. Maybe slides. Just don't tell him our bodies are 70 percent water!

CINKO'S NO THANKS LIST

NAUTICAL CHARTS

WATER BAGELS

WATER-MELONS

garden hoses

POOL TOYS

ICE-BAT ON A HOT DAY

MOVIE THEATER DRINKS

THE OLD MAN AND THE SEA

Poor Cinko is not really a big fan of anything wet. A lot of his time is spent worrying about water.

What if I get thirsty? What if we go on a field trip to the Sahara?

I Don't LIKE HORROR MOVIES.

8 GLASSES PER DAY!

HEALTH DEPT.

What if I get a job and the co-workers want to gossip?

What if I take my family to the drive-thru and they all order water?

TRY THE EXTRA-VALUE WATER MEAL!

100% UGLY BURGER

OTHER!

100% H2O

ORDER HERE

MENU: Burger: $$ WATER: FRE

FUN IN THE SUN & CINKO ON THE RUN AT: **UGLY BEACH**

There's nothing like getting a tan at the seashore. If you feel like lying around with nothing to worry about other than having sand kicked in your face and very expensive hot dogs, you've come to the right place.

SAND DOLLAR
SNACK N' PAY

SCUBA RENTAL & RESCUE

TACO = $1.00
SALAD = $1.00
CPR = $10,000.00

BURN

TOOT TOOT WHARF & FUN-FAIR PIER

Toot toot! Do you have your sea legs?
No worries . . . neither does the
captain of the Ugly Showboat.
If you're looking for a rocky climb up and down
the furious waves of the ugly seas, you've come
to the right place! The Toot Toot Wharf &
Fun-Fair Pier is the place to be . . . careful.

You'll be needing all 99 bottles of seasickness pills on the wall. There's a lot to do aboard the Ugly Showboat. Enjoy a quick game of Go Fish with your bunkmate, look out the window (deluxe cot only), or go up on deck and be put to work! Good times!

SUPER {-ISH} MARKET/TOY SHOP

The Super-ish Market/Toy Shop is where everyone goes for fresh fish, vegetables, water, and toys. Because Uglytown is so full of restaurants and busy business folks, the supermarket sales were a little slow . . . so they added a toy shop! Now you can get your crackers, dishwashing liquid, and set of talking sailor robots all at once.

The wait at the supermarket isn't that bad . . . about forty minutes to get your number and another hour to be called. Once you're called, you have a good chance of placing an order! All you have to do is get the attention of someone behind the counter. They're usually too busy calling numbers.

The baskets at the supermarket all have special wheels, so your shopping experience is always an adventure.

UGLYZOOLOGY
FILE 001

ICE·BAT

Everything Ice-Bat touches turns to ice. Yet he warms your heart. He's tons of fun to chill with and always a blast when you're just hanging around. Eh, you know, because bats sleep upside down.

He received high marks in flight school at an early age, but his true talents shine in sub-zero temperatures.

(A) WARMS YOUR HEART

(B) ICE-COLD!

(C) Just Chill?

Ice-Bat lives in an ice-box!
His sleepy, chilly home can be
transported around town
with the help of
Wage's Big Tow.

HE LIVES IN AN ICE-BOX!

True, things can get cold
to the touch when hanging
around with Ice-Bat,
but his sense of
humor is enough
to warm even
the coldest shoulder.

NOW THAT'S COLD

Just don't ask him if he melts.

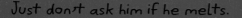

Just outside the walls of Uglytown, you can
enjoy camping and the great outdoors in the
Haunted Woods! Why are the woods haunted?
Mostly because that's what ghosts do . . .
haunt. It's a tough job, but someone's got to
do it, right? Afraid of ghosts? No problem!
Simply cower in fear, cover yourself up with
a blanket, and hide!

HAUNTED WOODS

CAMP GEAR CHECKLIST

- ☐ BEANS
- ☐ POTTY 2 GO
- ☐ GUIDE
- ☐ Doggie Tent
- ☐ BEAR REPELLENT
- ☐ Bug REPELLENT
- ☐ GHOST REPELLENT
- ☐ CAMP-FIRE
- ☐ AIR FRESHENER
- ☐ NO-SUCH-THING-AS-BIGFOOT NET
- ☐ Butterfly NET
- ☐ WAY OUT of ButterFly NET

It's a checklist, not a quiz! So no worries . . . there are no correct answers here.

Boo

KARAOKE night ♪

NOW that's JUST RUDE.

UGLY BEAUTY SHOP

WE HELP YOU HELP US HELP YOUR FACE

Welcome to the Ugly Beauty Shop!
Need a makeover? Then you've come to the
wrong place! But if you're happy with the way
you look, look no further. See, the way you look
on the outside is a reflection of how you're
feeling on the inside. That's why Target looks a
lot like a jelly donut.

The expert barbers at the Ugly Beauty Shop are
highly trained professionals. They use combs,
brushes, and toothbrushes. They have pretty much
anything you need to get the tangles untangled
and to make the three hairs you have left behave
the way you want them to. Hey, but what's with
the blue water?

surprise!

MIRROR

Some
Poofy
THING

The thing
with the
PINS!

THE
BLUE
WATER
THING!

WE MAKE YOU PRETTY UGLY

As you can see, the facility has been decorated to make even the most horrific transformations as painless as possible. If beauty is all in your mind, then so is the opinion that you've just received the worst haircut of your life!

PET-COSTUME EPICENTER

Everyone loves dress-up! There are many dress-up days and costume holidays in Uglytown. If you're in need of a costume, come on down to the Pet-Costume Epicenter! They have your size, know your style, and can make you look like everything from a chicken to a superhero. Or maybe a superchicken.

NOW WITH HIGH **PRICES**

PET

OK We're **OPEN**

HARD-WORKING PERSON

BUNNY

CHICKEN

PLANT

CROC

MONSTER

HEALTH FOOD

UGLY POLICE FORCE

There's not too much crime in Uglytown. But there's a lot of Ox and Wedgehead. The Ugly police force uses a special wagon to transport them from the bank, the bakery, or even local yard sales to the "time-out" room.

The police in Uglytown ride around on really neato motorbikes. That sidecar can eject!

Ox and Wedgehead are very familiar
with the Ugly holding tank.

The police are always ready to act. By car or
boat or even on foot, the law is ready to catch
you! Uh, help you.

Moxy has a lot of moxie. She has an unlimited source of energy and doesn't know when to stop! Her brother, Ox, has become an expert at using this type of energy to win the Ugly marathon (with a bike), much to the dismay of the other Uglys, who love sticking to the rules of fair play. There are two or three of them. We think. Maybe.

UGLY BANK

& LUNCH HUT

Bank on it! The Ugly Bank is where you keep everything from your family fortune to your family misfortune nice and safe. Have some gold? Put it in the Ugly Bank! Have some rare coins? Make a deposit! Have some cookies? Please share.

MAKE A DEPOSIT

☐ BIG MONEY   ☐ COIN CHANGE   ☐ LINT   ☐ STRING

MAGIC?

We turn your dollar into OUR DOLLAR.

One thing's for certain: the line at the Ugly Bank is LONG!!! Perfect! Plenty of time for some burgers from the Bank 'n' Chew Line Lunch Hut. And after lunch you can take a nice long nap. We wish you pleasant dreams (of being next).

All hotel rooms look the same with the lights out, right?

So why spend your perfectly good shopping money on super deluxe hotels? Most travelers to Uglytown stay at the Hotel de la Feo.

Why does the hotel look run-down? Hey, you have it all wrong. We call that "character" here in Uglytown. The Hotel de la Feo has tons of character. Especially in the bathrooms!

Each room has a special theme. This room is great for when you don't really want to sleep. The nice springs in the mattress guarantee you'll be up all night!

The bellhops here are as creative as they are helpful.

I have a new workout VIDEO CALLED "GET YOUR OWN BAGS"!

LET US KNOW IF YOU NEED MORE:

☐ TOILET PAPER

☐ SOAP

☐ TOWELS

☐ RAT CATCHER 2000

Jeero is a dreamer. He's always dreamed of owning the ultimate relax chair. He realized that the twenty-four-hour Super Mart around the corner has these chairs on the sales floor for anyone to try out! And they have potato chips just a few aisles over!

☐ CHIPS

☐ DIP

☐ DIPSTICK

Now Jeero spends most of his time in a state of suspended animation in the electronics relax-chair demo area at Super Mart. It isn't that he's lazy. He's just a really careful shopper. Just when he's ready to decide on a new TV and relax chair, the new models come out and he has to start all over again.

Something like that.

JEERO'S MUST-HAVES

ANCIENT TECHNOLOGY

OLD-FASHIONED FIREPLACE

EXERCISE EQUIPMENT

GUARD-DOG BRIBE

SUPER MART NIGHT KEY

WORKOUT VIDEO

UGLY HISTORY MUSEUM

To understand the present, you must look to the past! Why is Security chasing you? Because a few minutes ago, you walked into the museum without buying a ticket! Anyway, the Ugly History Museum is where you can find many excuses for why things are the way they are today!

So is the horse #4?

4 FATHERS

The Uglys are very interested in history.
Where did they come from? How do they
get home? The answers are out there.

UGLYCARS

If you're into cars, or anything strange, you'll love the vehicles of Uglytown. Every automobile in town has a special theme and style as unique as the Ugly driving it! From Wage's Big Tow to the Now You Sea Food mobile, you're bound to catch sight of some truly odd autos here and there. Well, everywhere.

Each and every car is custom-built!
What a waste of money . . . but what fun!

Uglytown has everything
you need, and everything you
would never need but now want real bad!

The Uglyverse is filled with funny little nooks and crannies to explore. Keep in mind that all things are possible, and that if you believe in yourself, you will make your dreams come true! When that happens, please spend your dream money here.
It's good for tourism.

BYE

OK BYE

SLEEPY
Night Night

SEE YA

LYCON

ALWAYS
CLOSED

What you need is an UGLY GUIDE

what dat?

UGLY GUIDE

Have you spent your whole life in search of the guide that will improve your mind, win you friends, and make you tons of money? Well, too bad. You'll just have to take this Ugly Guide instead! This Ugly Guide may not make you smart, popular, or rich, but it is guaranteed to unlock the secrets of the Uglyverse, such as:

• Who has been spending so much time in the Ugly police force "time-out" room?

• What is with the blue water thing at the Ugly Beauty Shop?

• When does Ice-Bat retire to his ice-box?

• Where does Jeero spend most of his time in a state of suspended animation?

• Why should you care?

Because UGLY is the new beautiful!

POE'S CAVE COVE

ICE FACTORY

OK

STOR

UGL
TOW

CREEPY SHACK

UGLY FARM & LANDING PLATFORM

ZOO
& PASTRY SHOP
FACTORY

CAS
FE

X

THE KNOWN UGLYVERSE

THIS WAY

THAT WAY

HAUNTED CAMP WOODS

FUN PIER

MT. FEO

UGLY DRAGON MT.

DAVID HORVATH and SUN-MIN KIM are a husband-and-wife team living in Los Angeles with their daughter, Mina. They met in art school in New York, where they began creating and designing art and toys together. Their relationship continued to grow, and the Uglydolls™ were born in 2001, quickly becoming a worldwide success with fans of all ages. The Uglydolls™ appeal to everyone, from children to toy collectors to art enthusiasts. David, Sun-Min, and the Uglydolls™ family (twenty-four characters and still growing) have won the Toy of the Year Award and have been featured on CNN, MSNBC, and the Today show and in the New York Times, InStyle, Time magazine, and store windows around the world. You can find the creators every year at the annual Uglycon fan convention, where they will be happy to talk about their continuing adventures in the Uglyverse.

EATS HOMEWORK?
- ☐ with salt.
- ☐ HE DOES TAKEOUT.

ICE-BAT IS MADE OF ICE?
- ☐ Heart of gold.
- ☐ MADE OF MONEY!

He needs...
- ☐ His mommy.
- ☐ MORE!

This is....
- ☐ business as usual.
- ☐ typical!

- ☐ Bigger!
- ☐ More chips!

- ☐ Bye bye, teeth.
- ☐ Now we're talkin'!

TESTY QUIZ

There are no right answers!

THIS IS WAGE
- ☐ TRUE.
- ☐ WHATEVER YOU SAY, PAL.
- ☐ SOME of him.

BABO LIKES COOKIES?
- ☐ ALWAYS.
- ☐

OX RHYMES with...
- ☐ BIG MONEY.
- ☐ A MICROPHONE.

This shop is...
- ☐ Just ok.
- ☐ NOT SO BAD!

IF wedgehead drops his train ticket and it cost $40, how fast will he have to run from Ox?
- ☐ Too Late.
- ☐ OX left, too bad!

UGLY

SPECIAL CARD

NAME: _____
AGE: _____
LIKES: _____
NO THANKS: _____

Don't clip! You'll ruin it!!!

This Ugly Guide is merely a guide.
Okay, I mean, you knew that already.
What we really mean is, you are UGLY!
Aha, but what does UGLY mean?
UGLY means celebrating
who you are on the inside and
showing us what you've got!

WHEN YOU READ, CHECK YOUR

CHECKLIST

UGLY GUIDE

Ak!!

☐ Book   ☐ LIGHT   ☐ BOOKMARK

US $5.99 / $7.50 CAN
ISBN 978-0-375-84275-7

50599

9 780375 842757

Random House
www.randomhouse.com/kids
www.uglydollbooks.com

Sun❤️in DAVID